I Can Read!

2 WITH HELP

P9-DFA-661

WONDER WOMAN

MEET THE HEROES

Adapted by
Steve Korté
pictures by Lee Ferguson
colors by Jeremy Roberts

Wonder Woman created by
William Moulton Marston

HARPER
An Imprint of HarperCollinsPublishers

HEROES IN THIS BOOK:

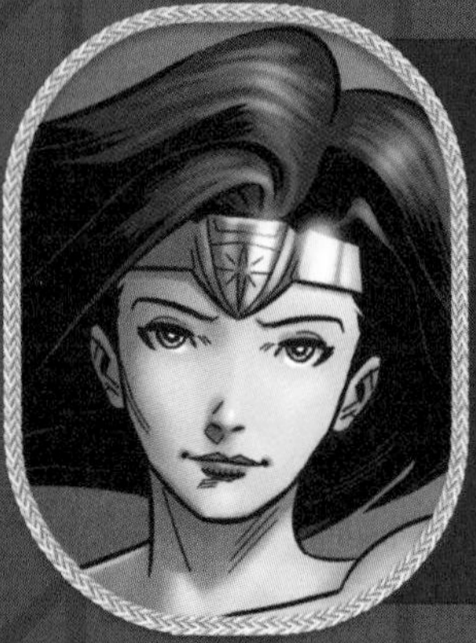

DIANA PRINCE / WONDER WOMAN

Born on the island of Themyscira, Diana is an Amazon princess. She trained with the other Amazons to become a warrior, and when she was ready, she joined our world to bring peace to mankind.

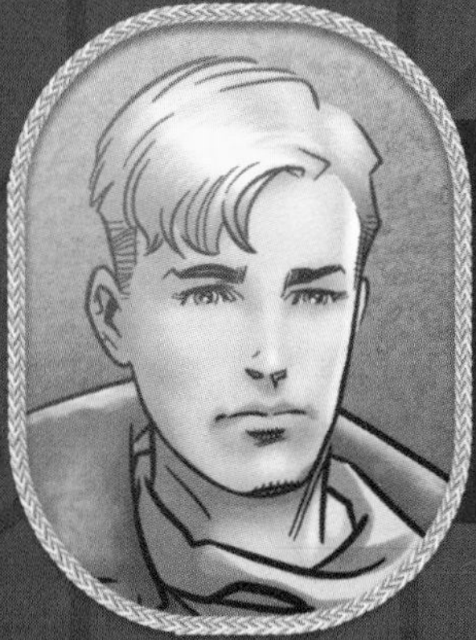

STEVE TREVOR

Steve Trevor is the first man to set foot on the island of Themyscira. He brought Diana to his world to help stop the war.

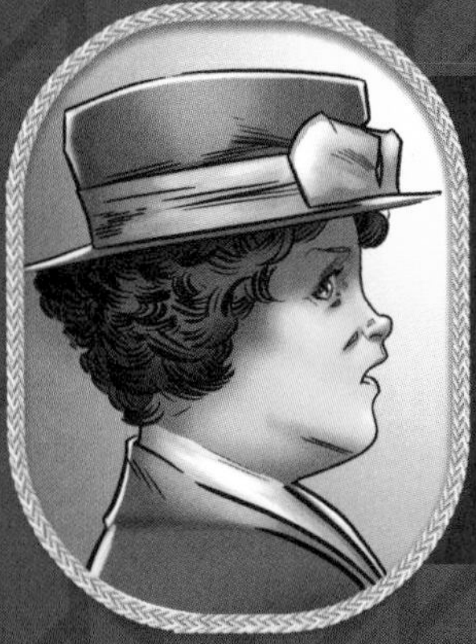

ETTA CANDY

Etta is Steve Trevor's secretary. She helps Diana learn how to fit in when she arrives in London, and she aids the heroes as they go off to fight in the war.

Dear Parent:
Your child's love of reading starts here!

Every child learns to read in a different way and at his or her own speed. Some go back and forth between reading levels and read favorite books again and again. Others read through each level in order. You can help your young reader improve and become more confident by encouraging his or her own interests and abilities. From books your child reads with you to the first books he or she reads alone, there are I Can Read Books for every stage of reading:

SHARED READING
Basic language, word repetition, and whimsical illustrations, ideal for sharing with your emergent reader

BEGINNING READING
Short sentences, familiar words, and simple concepts for children eager to read on their own

READING WITH HELP
Engaging stories, longer sentences, and language play for developing readers

READING ALONE
Complex plots, challenging vocabulary, and high-interest topics for the independent reader

ADVANCED READING
Short paragraphs, chapters, and exciting themes for the perfect bridge to chapter books

I Can Read Books have introduced children to the joy of reading since 1957. Featuring award-winning authors and illustrators and a fabulous cast of beloved characters, I Can Read Books set the standard for beginning readers.

A lifetime of discovery begins with the magical words "I Can Read!"

Visit www.icanread.com for information
on enriching your child's reading experience.

Wonder Woman: Meet the Heroes
Copyright © 2017 DC Comics.
WONDER WOMAN and all related characters and elements © & ™ DC Comics.
(s17)

HARP38973
Printed in the United States of America.
No part of this book may be used or reproduced in any manner whatsoever without written permission except
in the case of brief quotations embodied in critical articles and reviews. For information address HarperCollins
Children's Books, a division of HarperCollins Publishers, 195 Broadway, New York, NY 10007.
www.icanread.com

Library of Congress catalog card number: 2017932847
ISBN 978-0-06-268186-7

Book design by Erica De Chavez
17 18 19 20 21   LSCC   10 9 8 7 6 5 4 3 2 1
❖
First Edition

HIPPOLYTA

Hippolyta is the queen of the
Amazons and also Diana's mother.
She is a skilled warrior, a wise ruler,
and a loving mother.

ANTIOPE

Antiope is the general of the Amazons
and trained Diana in the art of combat.
She is also Queen Hippolyta's sister.

A young woman arrived in London.
She was excited to see the city.
She'd come from a faraway island.
Her name was Diana,
and she was on a mission
to save the world.
Her new friend, Steve Trevor,
walked beside her.
He was a captain in the army.

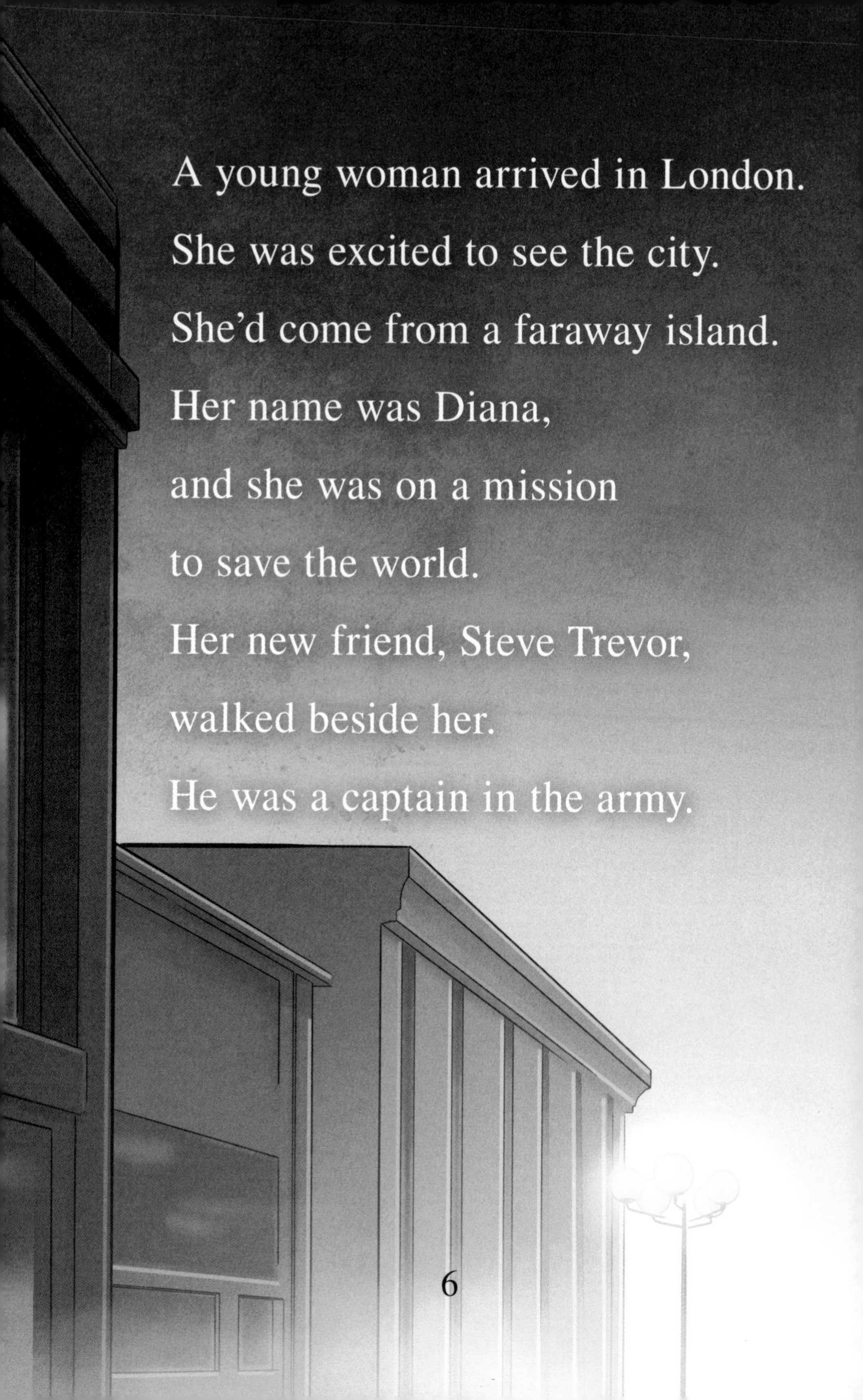

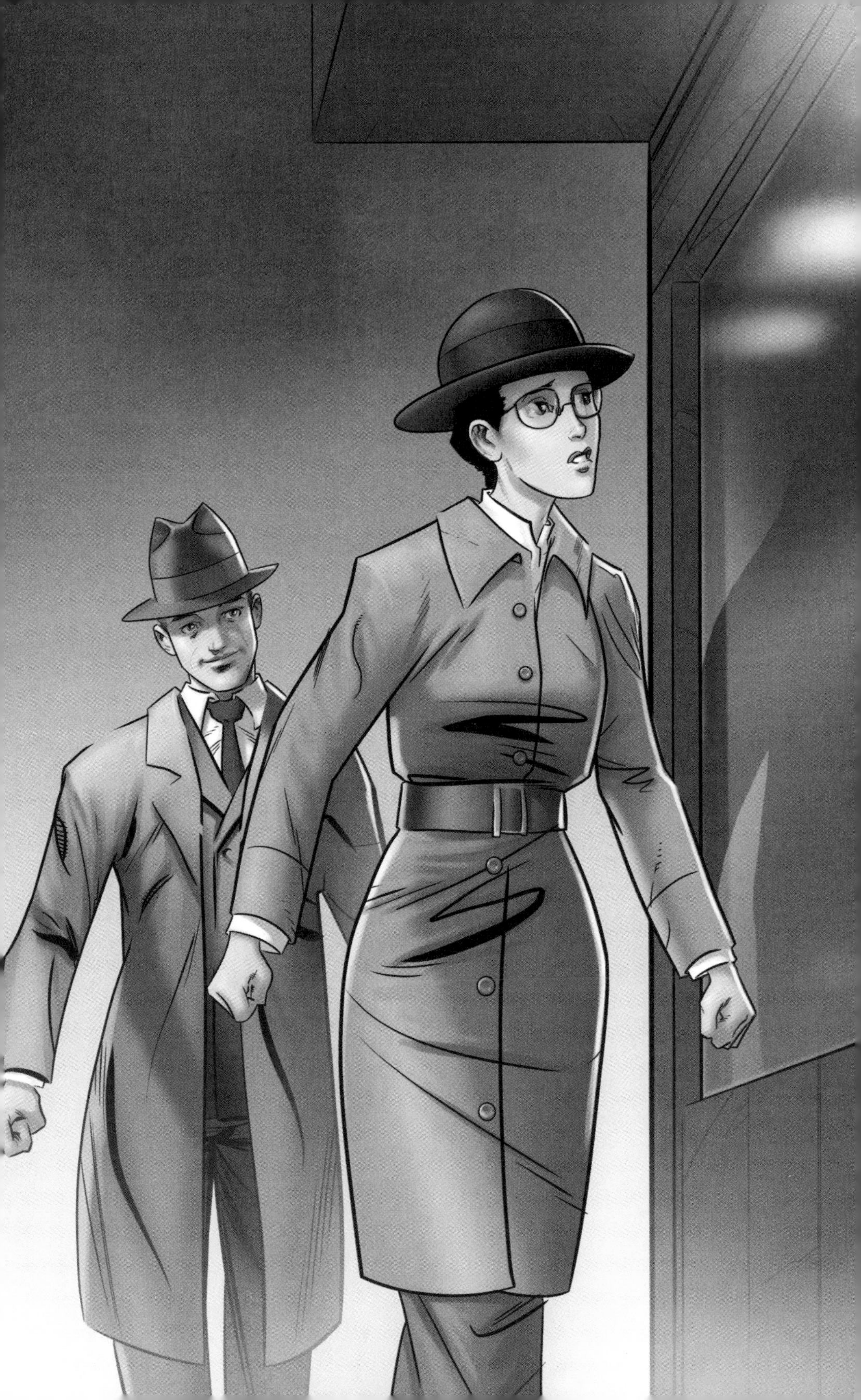

Suddenly, five men surrounded them.

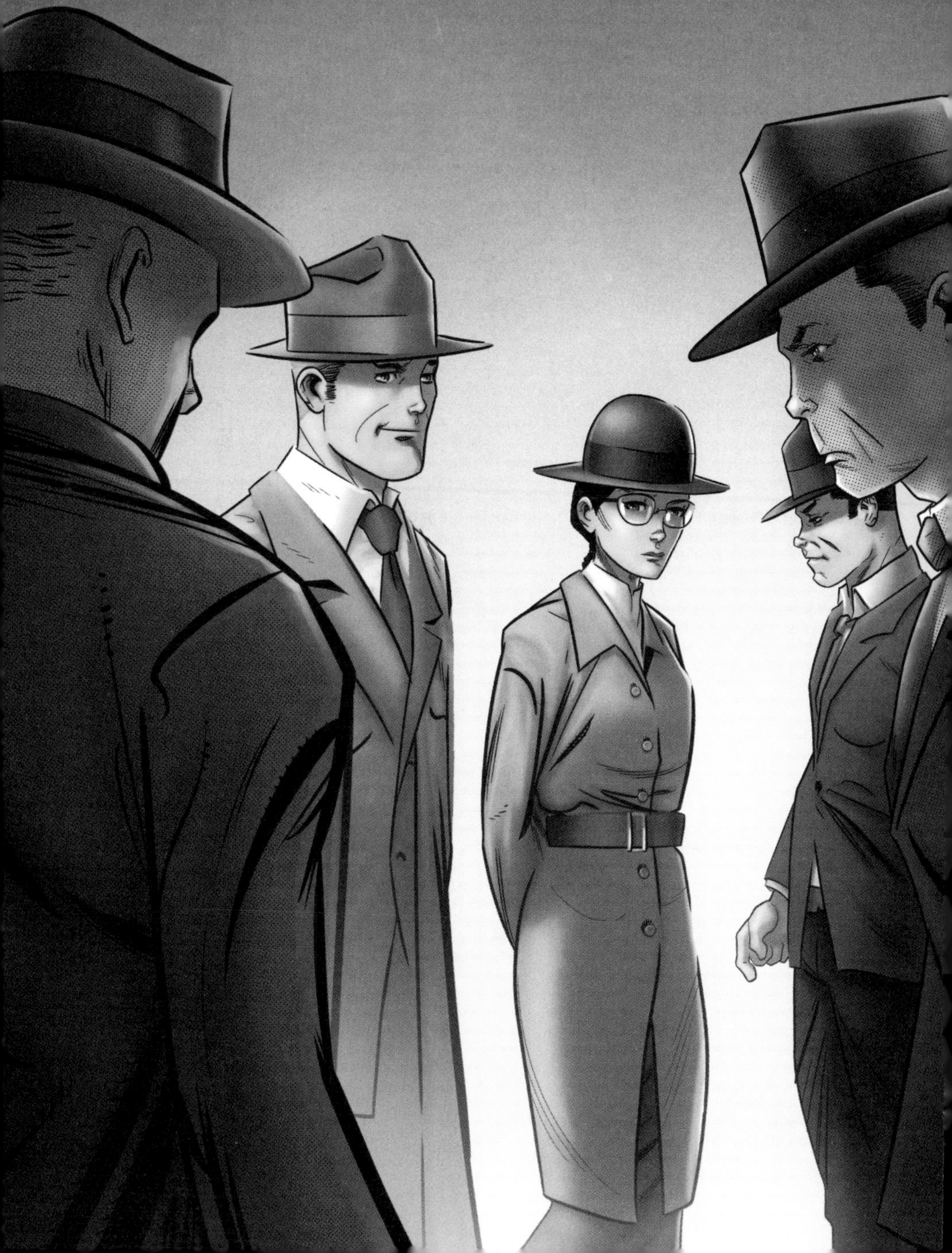

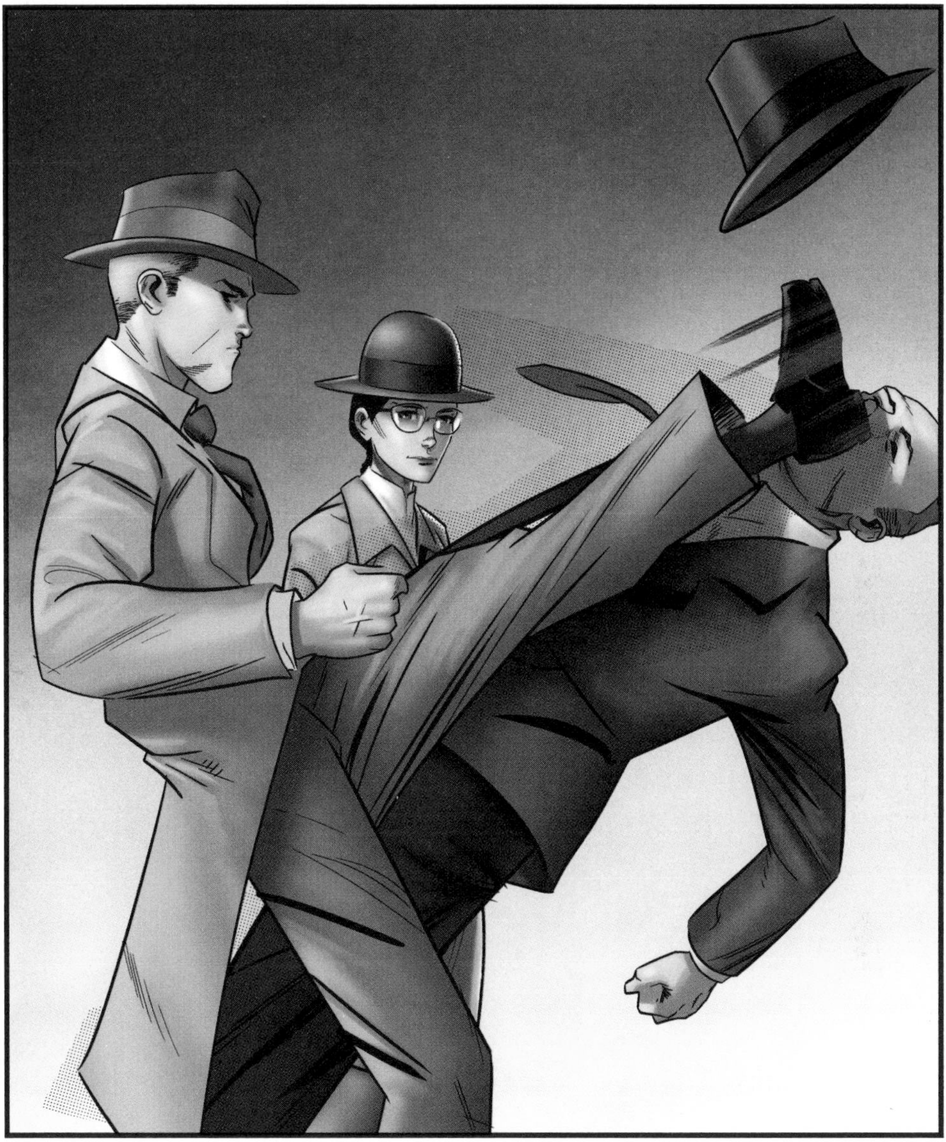

Steve stepped in front of Diana.

"Stay behind me!" he said to her.

He kicked one of the spies

to the ground.

Diana jumped forward.
She lifted one of the men
and swung him through the air.
He crashed into two
of the other men.
The fifth one quickly ran.
"He's getting away," said Steve.

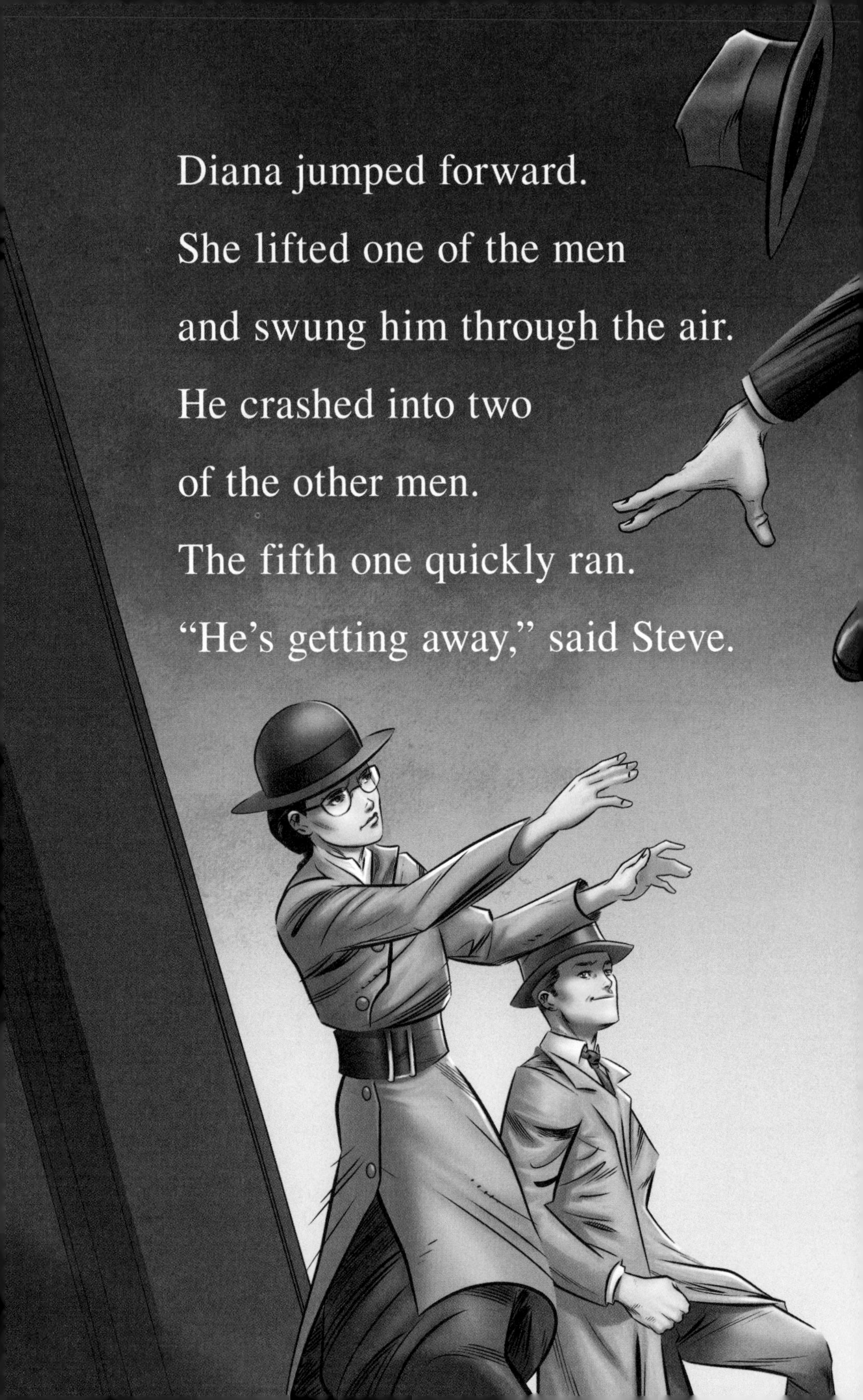

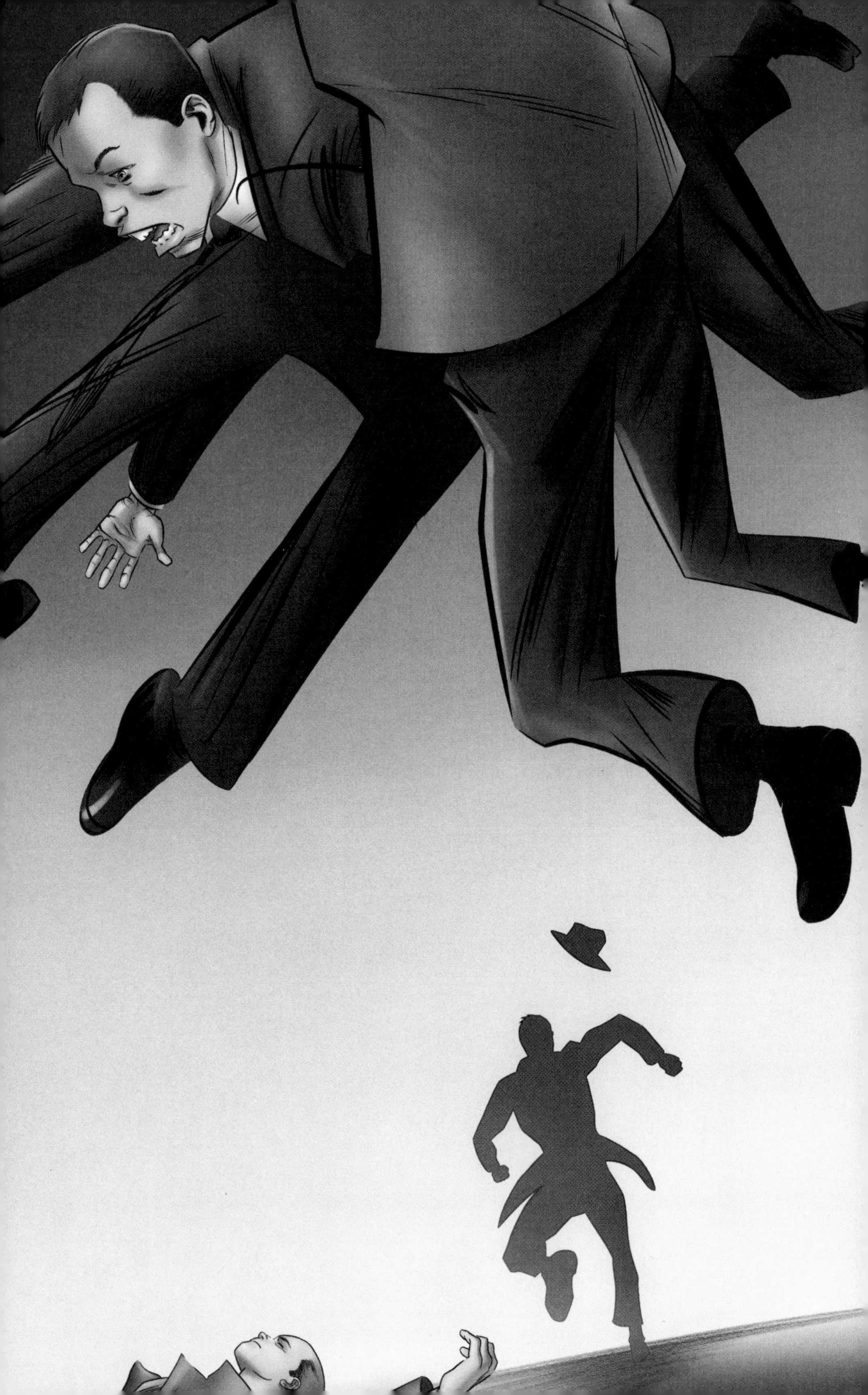

Steve and Diana followed the man.
They turned a corner.
The man was waiting for them.
Diana quickly pulled a sword from
under her coat and tripped him.

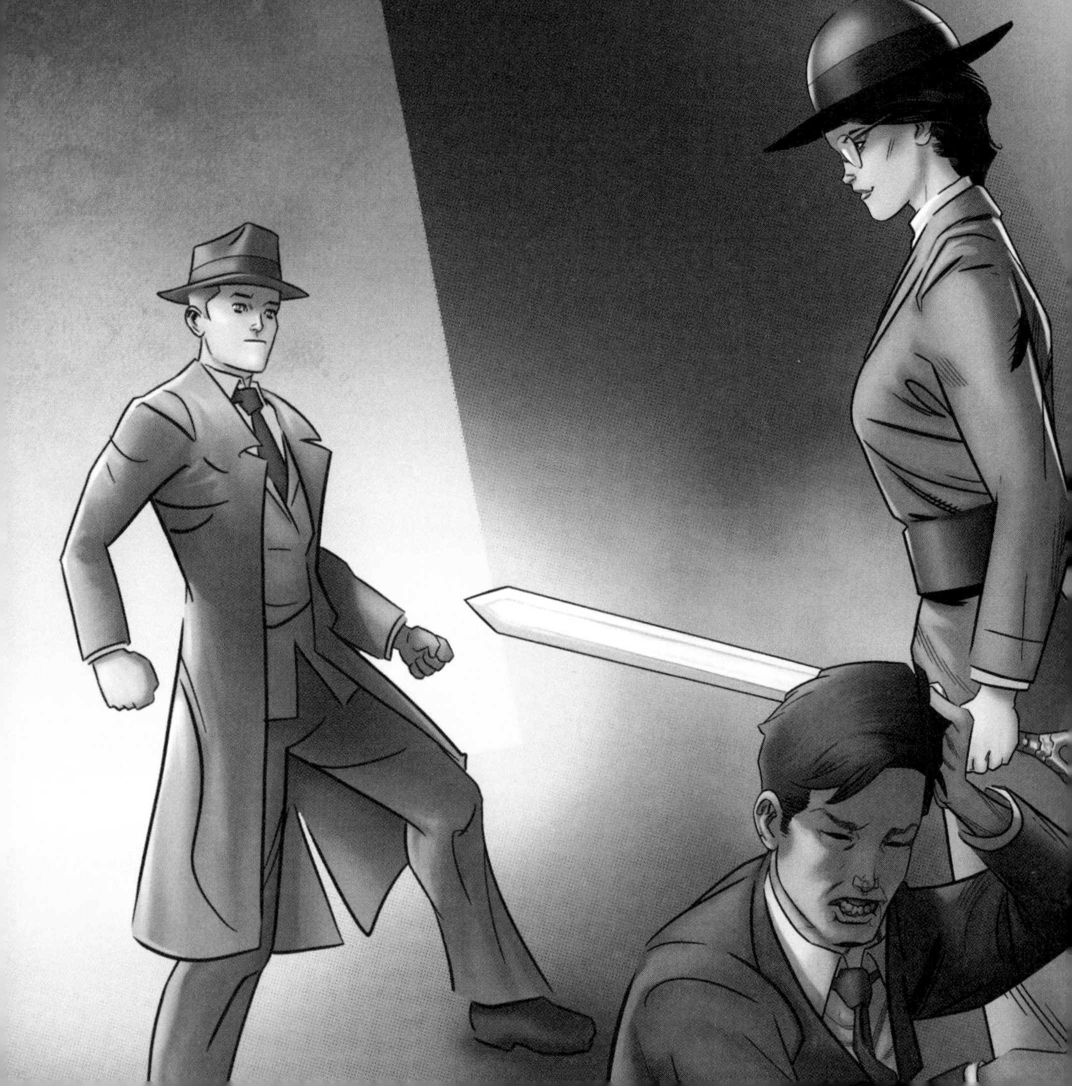

The sword belonged to Diana.

She had brought it from her home.

Diana smiled as she thought about

her home and her family.

They had prepared her

for her mission in London.

Long before Diana was born,

the Greek gods created

a race of wise women.

They were known as the Amazons.

They lived on a secret island

where no one could find them.

The Amazons trained every day

to become strong warriors.

Hippolyta was their queen,

and she was wise and kind.

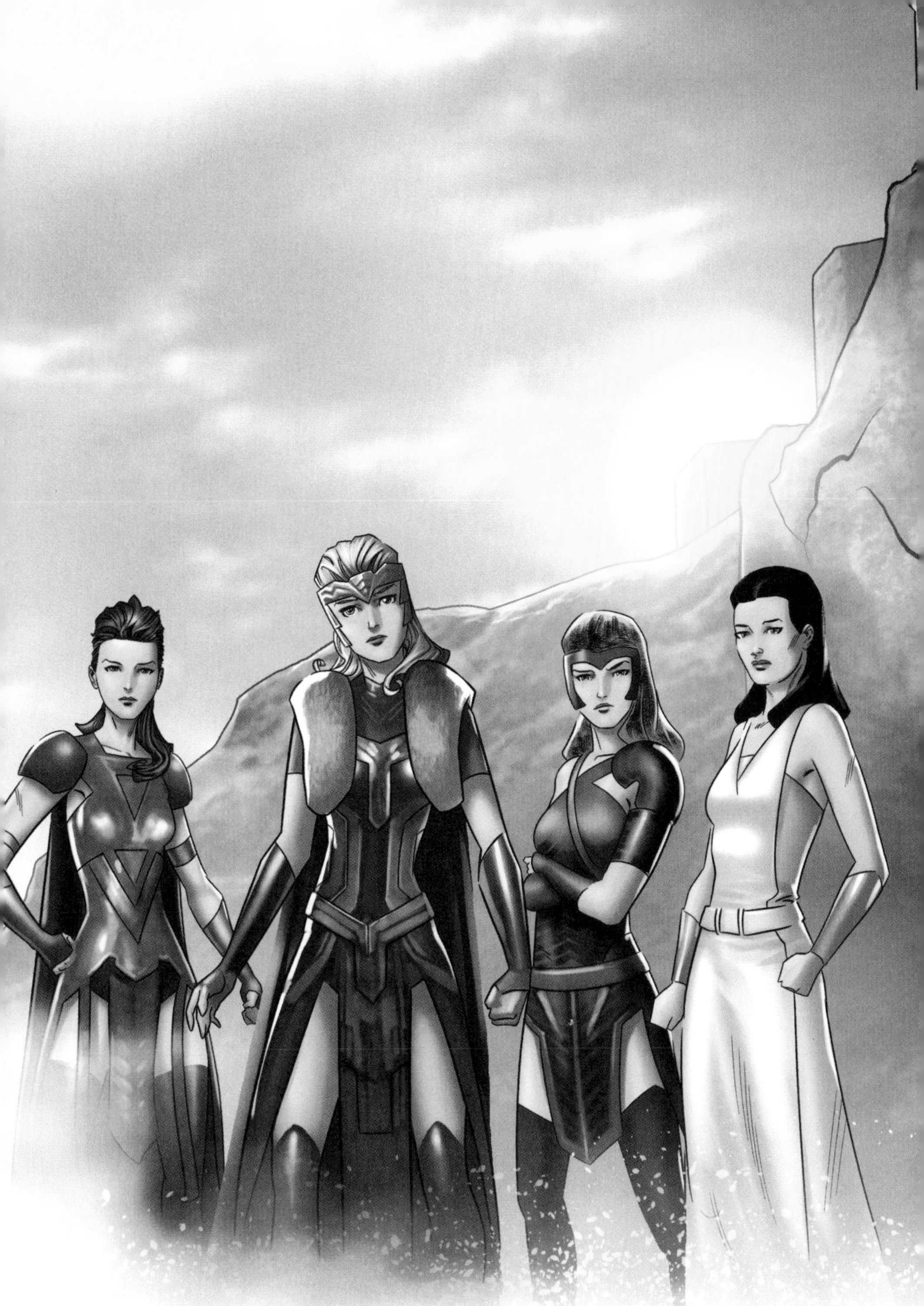

Diana was the daughter
of Queen Hippolyta.

She watched the Amazons train.

General Antiope was the leader
of the Amazon army.

Diana watched and learned.

By the time she was grown,

Diana was one of the

most skilled of the Amazons.

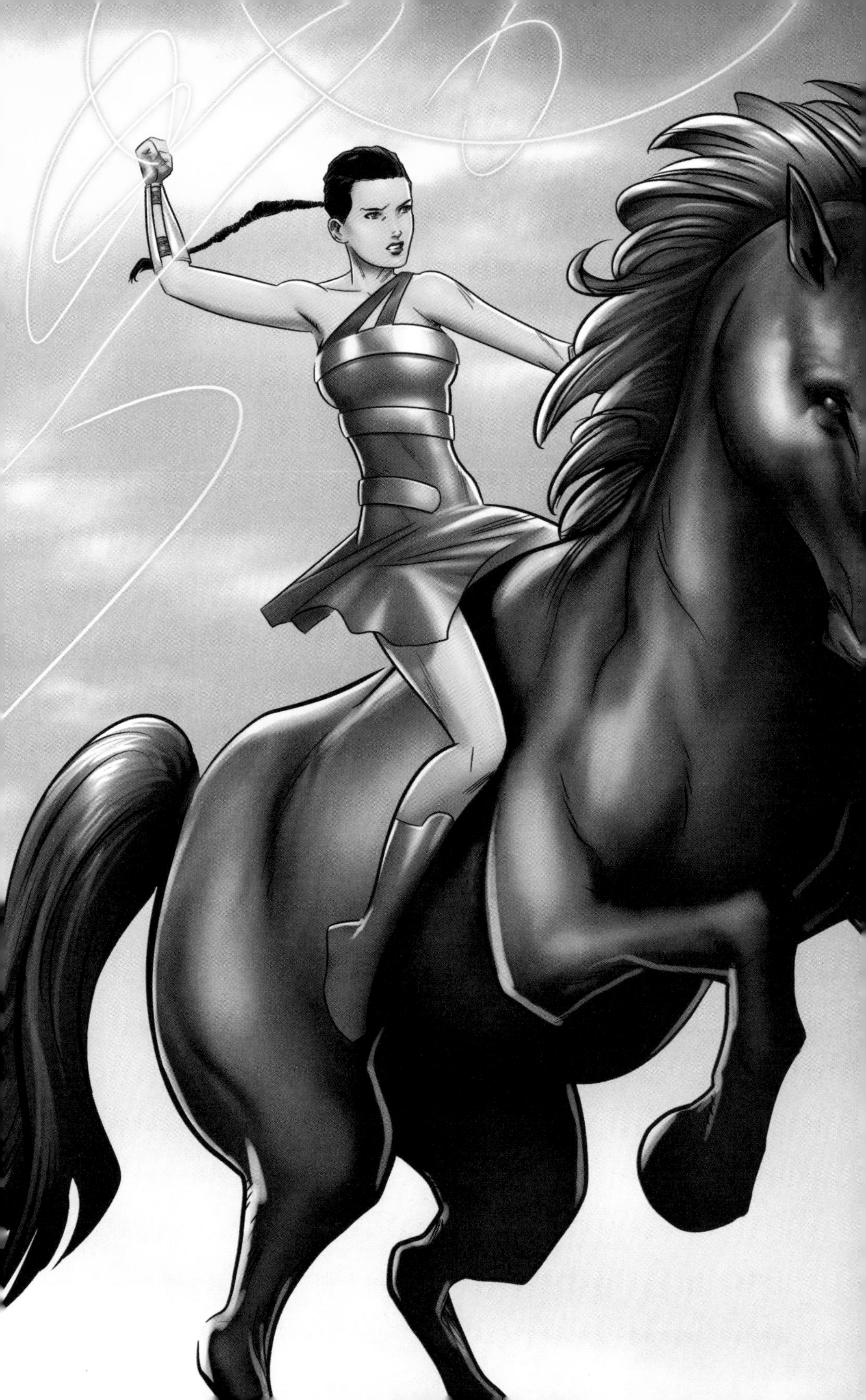

One day, a strange noise
filled the air.
Diana ran to the shore
of the island.
She watched an airplane
crash into the ocean.

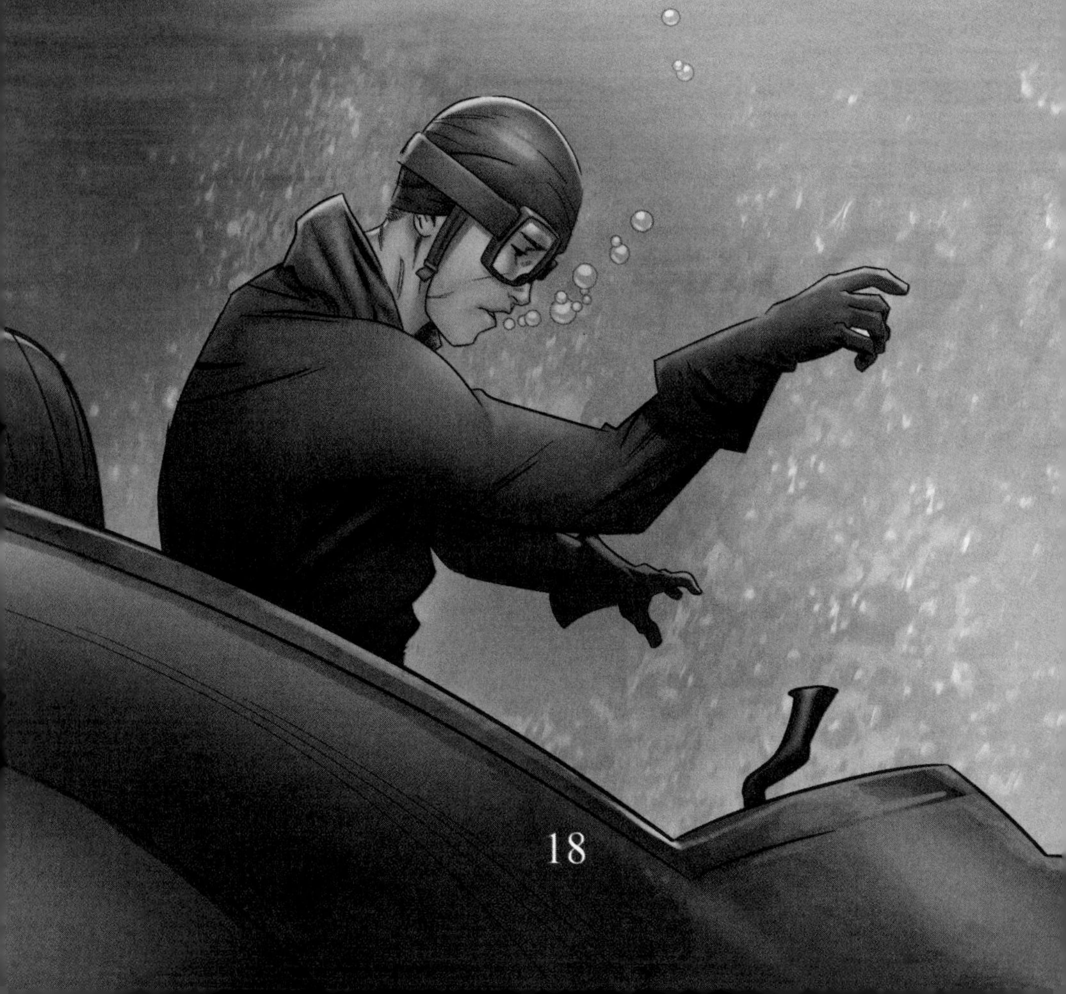

Diana jumped into the water
and rescued the pilot.
His name was Steve Trevor.
He was an American soldier
and the first man
Diana had ever seen.

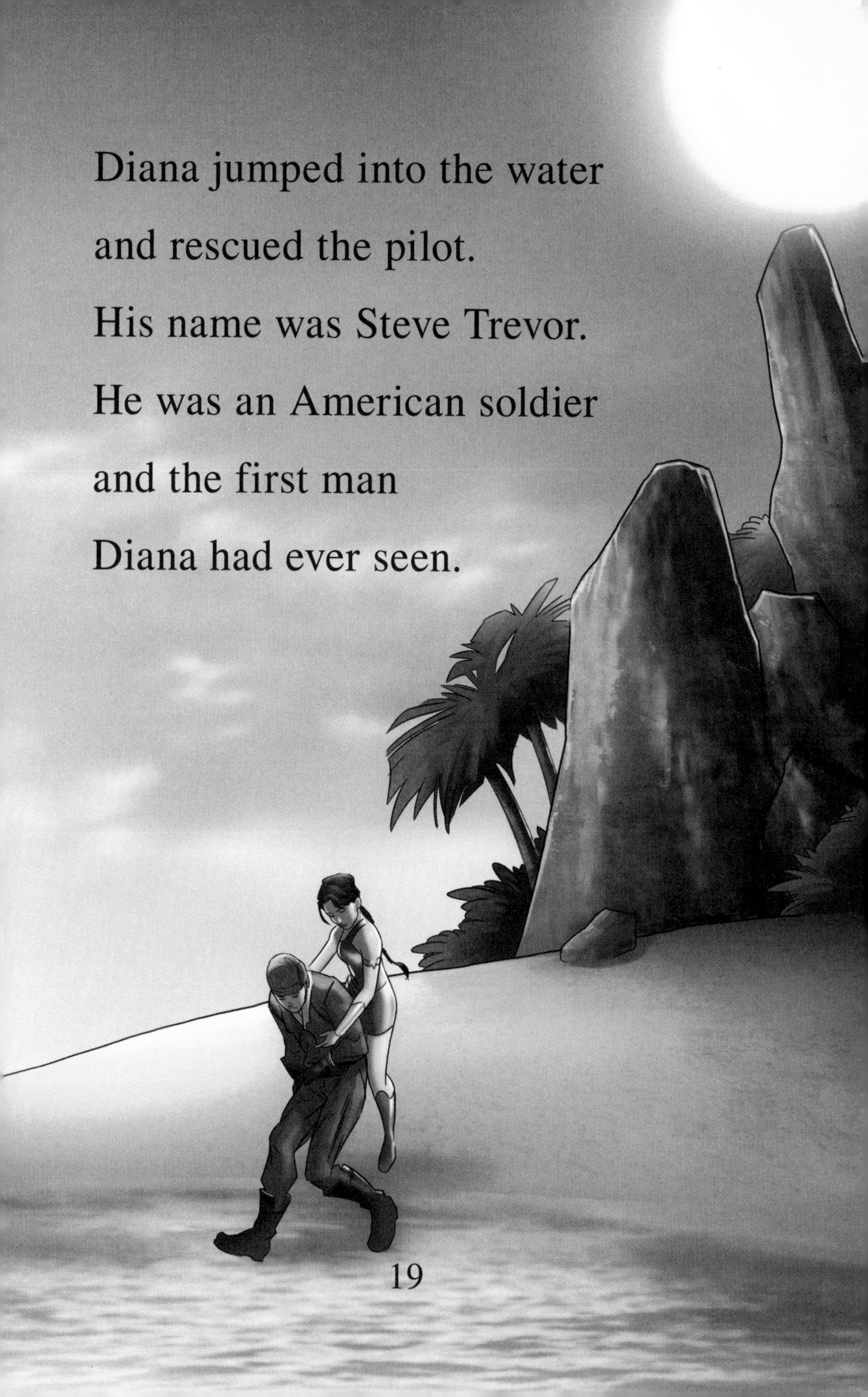

Steve told Diana and the Amazons
about a war that was spreading
in his world.

Diana spoke with her mother.

"Mankind needs our help.
It is our duty to defend
the world!" she said.

The queen was worried about her
daughter leaving the island.

"Be careful, Diana," she said.

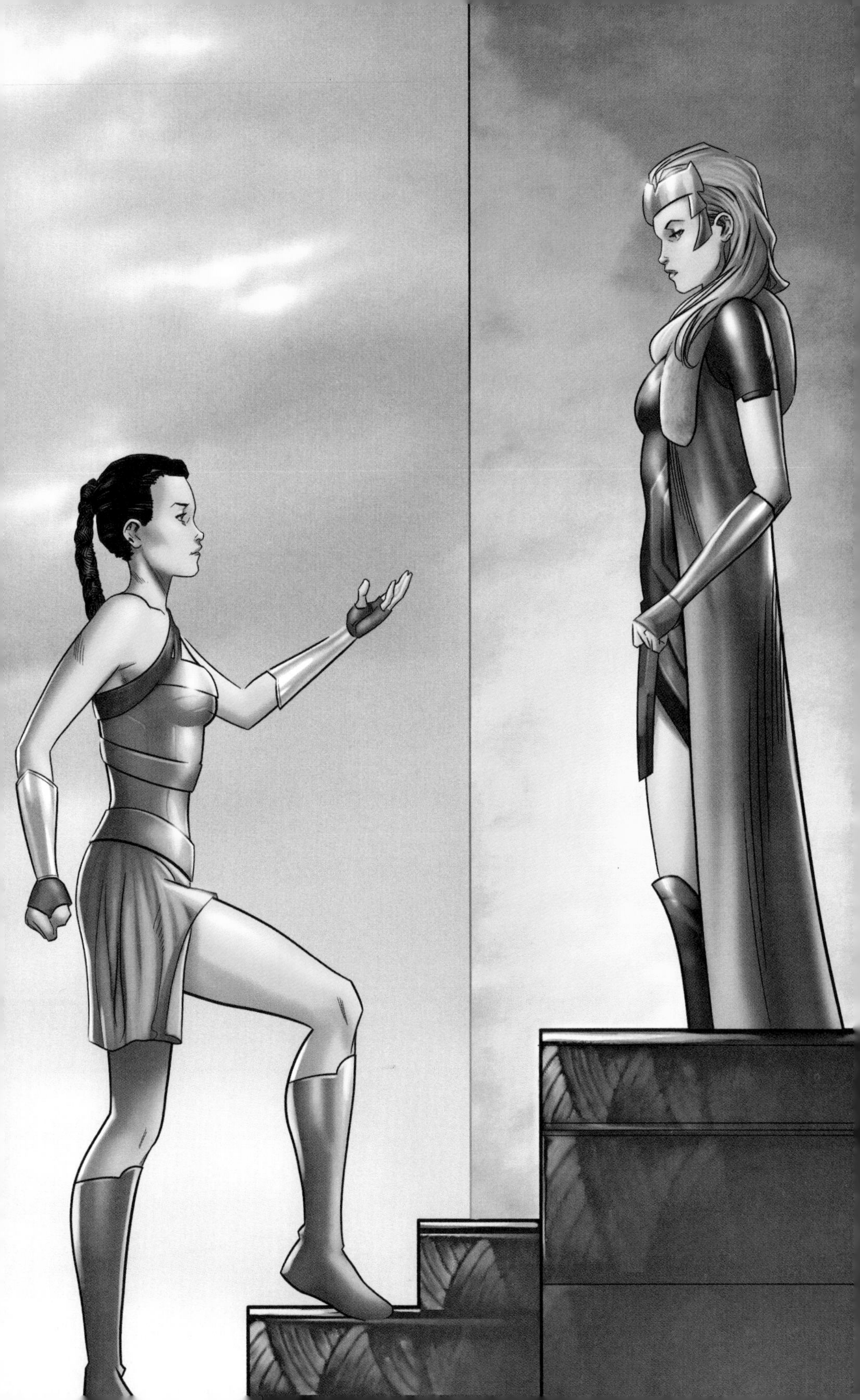

Diana decided to go with Steve
to fight in the war.
She put on a suit of Amazon armor.
Then she took a sword
and a magic lasso that would
force anyone to tell the truth.
Diana was powerful and kind.
She wanted to help the world.
Diana and Hippolyta said good-bye.

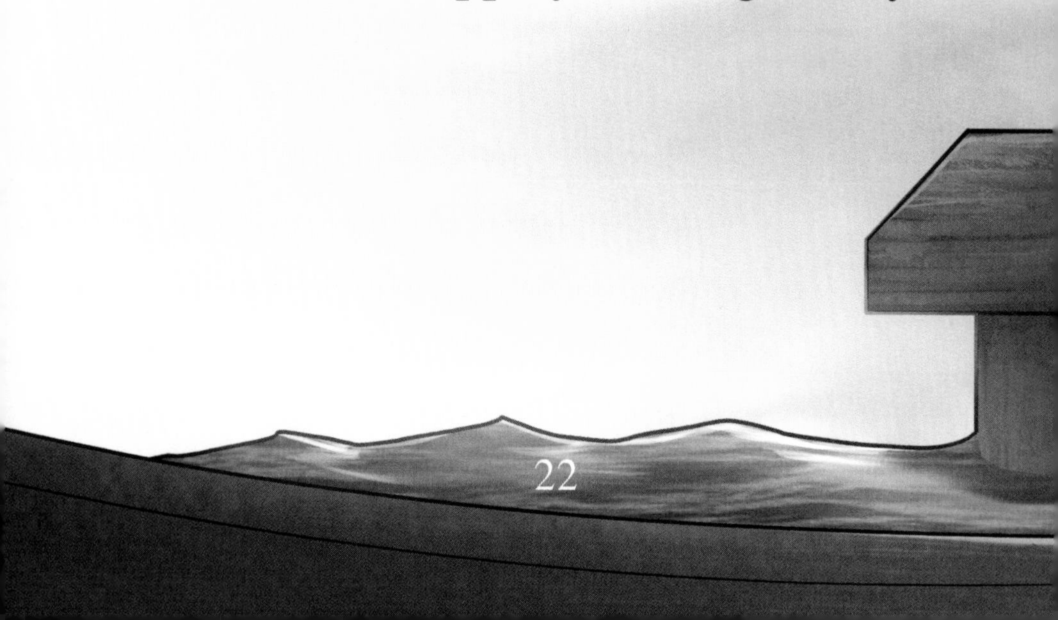

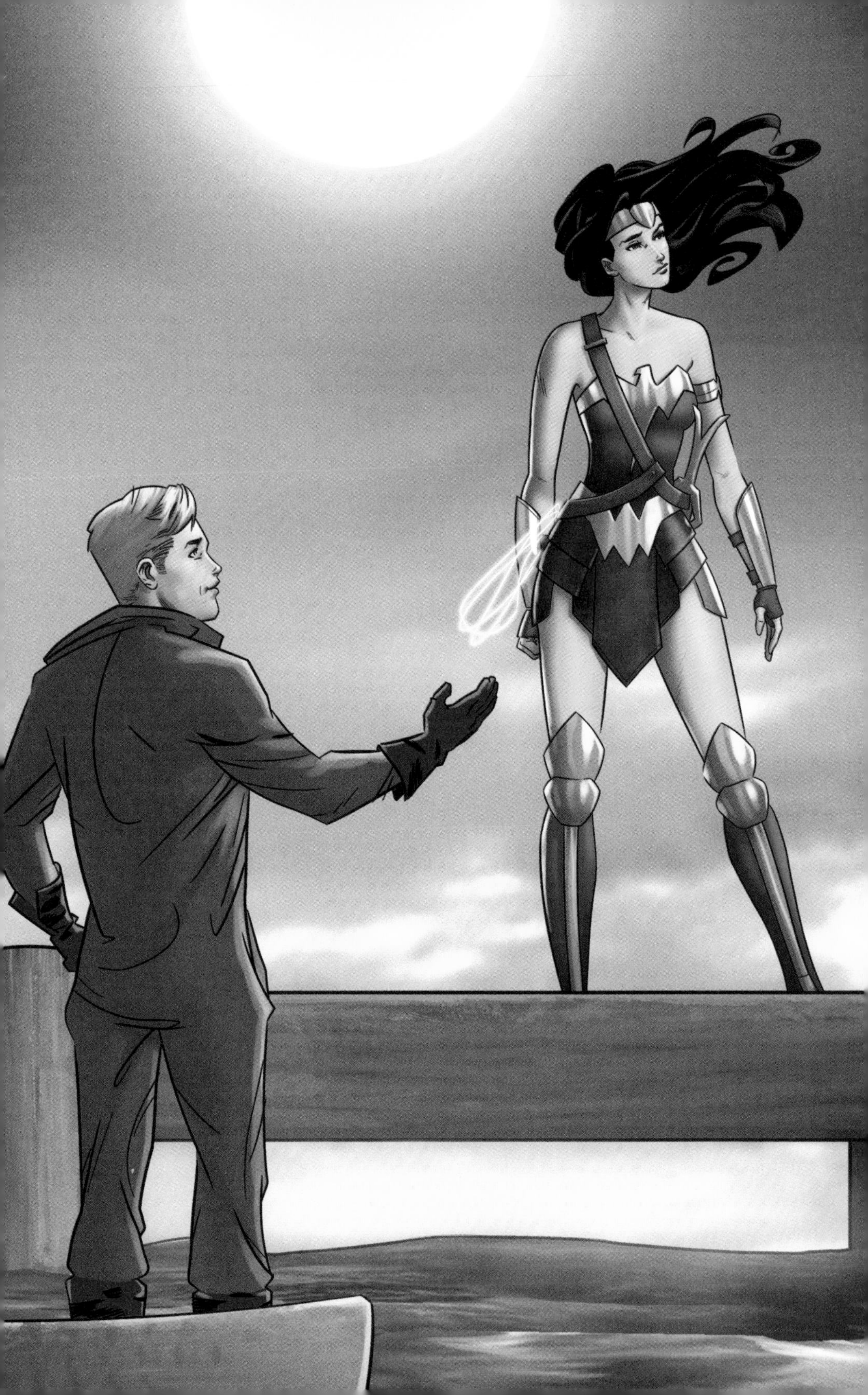

When they arrived in London,

a woman named Etta

helped Diana find new clothes.

She worked with Steve.

"How can a woman possibly fight

in this dress?" asked Diana.

She was different

from other women.

But she and Steve made a good team.

They had to get to the battle

to stop the enemy.

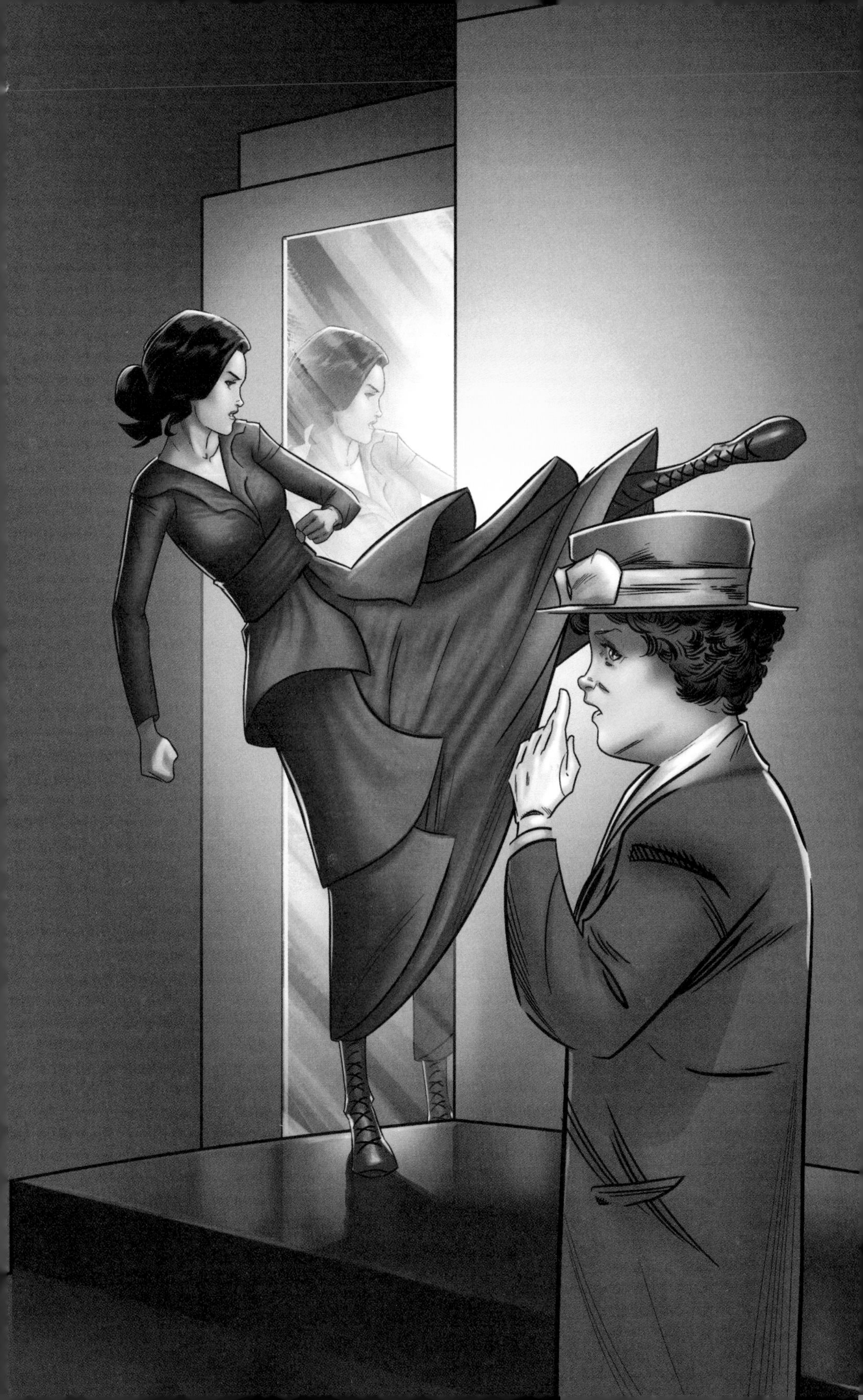

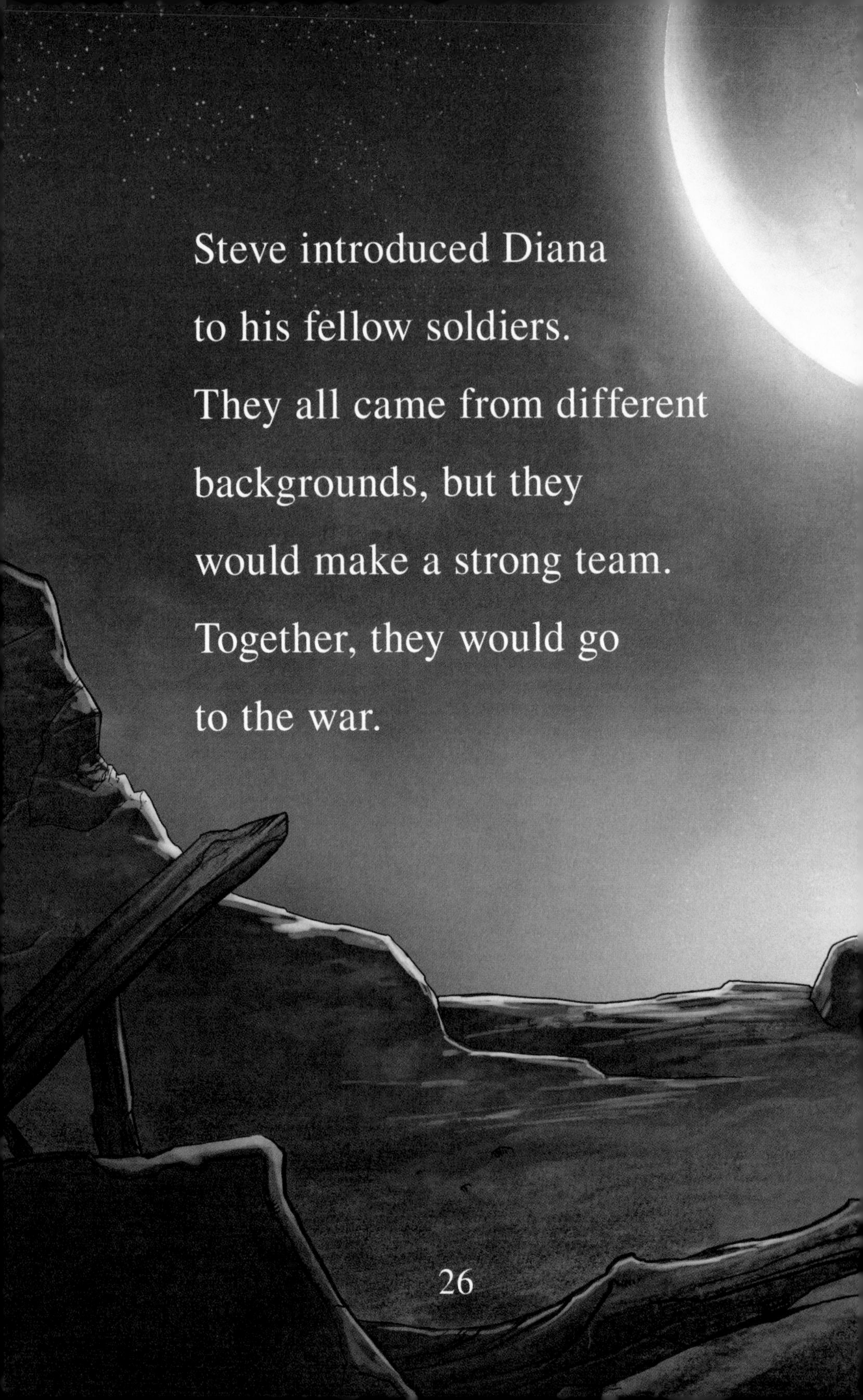

Steve introduced Diana to his fellow soldiers. They all came from different backgrounds, but they would make a strong team. Together, they would go to the war.

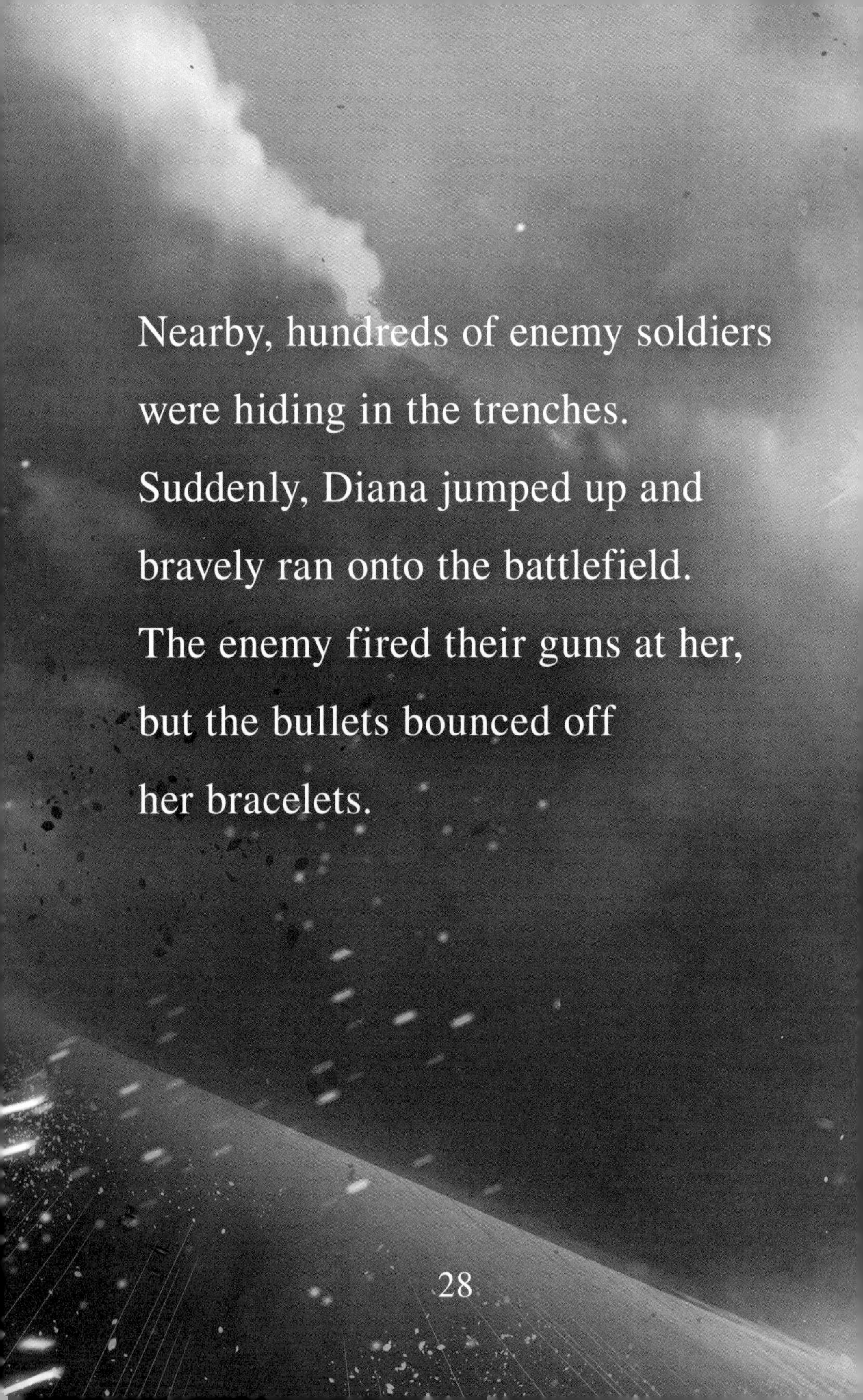

Nearby, hundreds of enemy soldiers were hiding in the trenches. Suddenly, Diana jumped up and bravely ran onto the battlefield. The enemy fired their guns at her, but the bullets bounced off her bracelets.

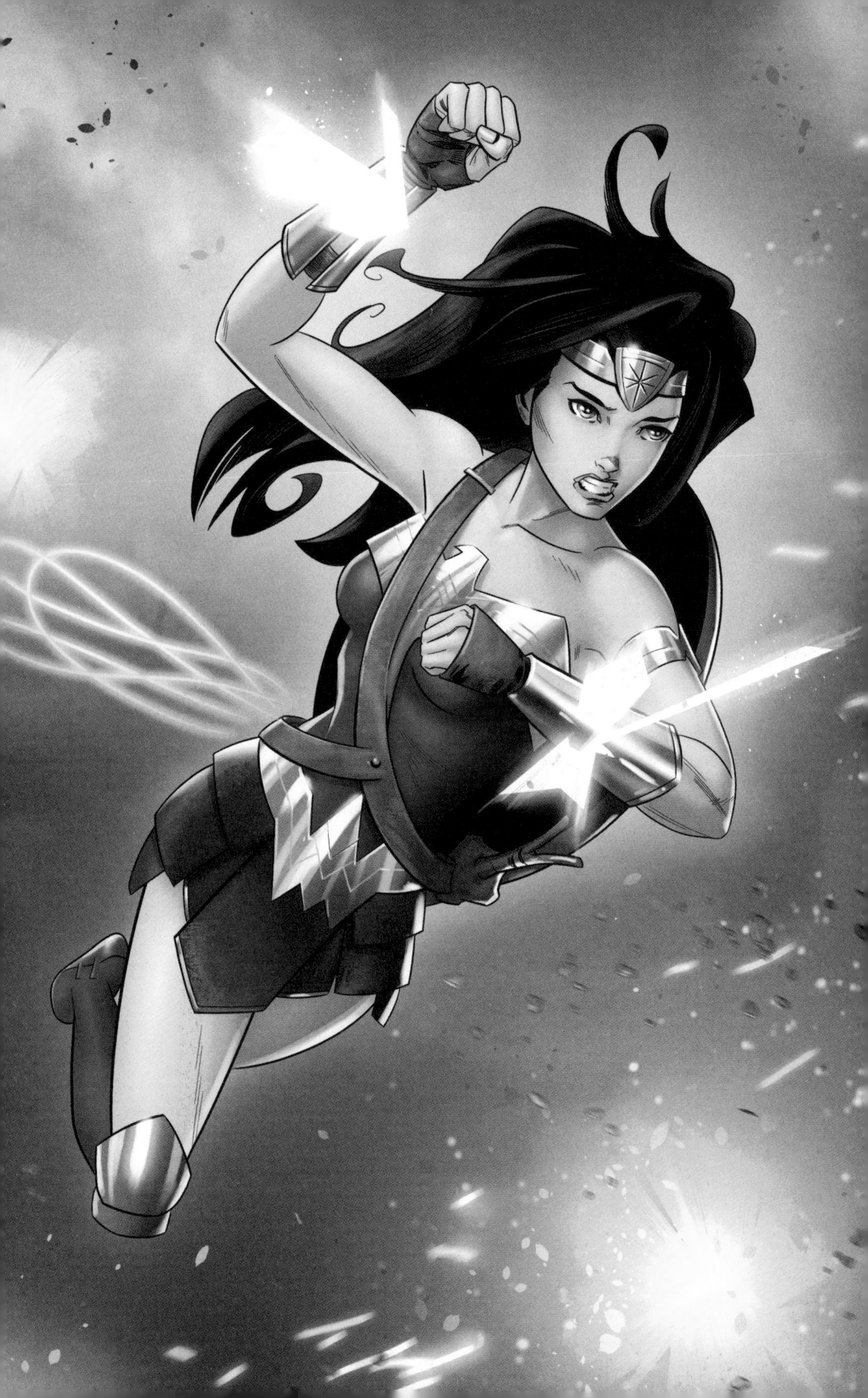

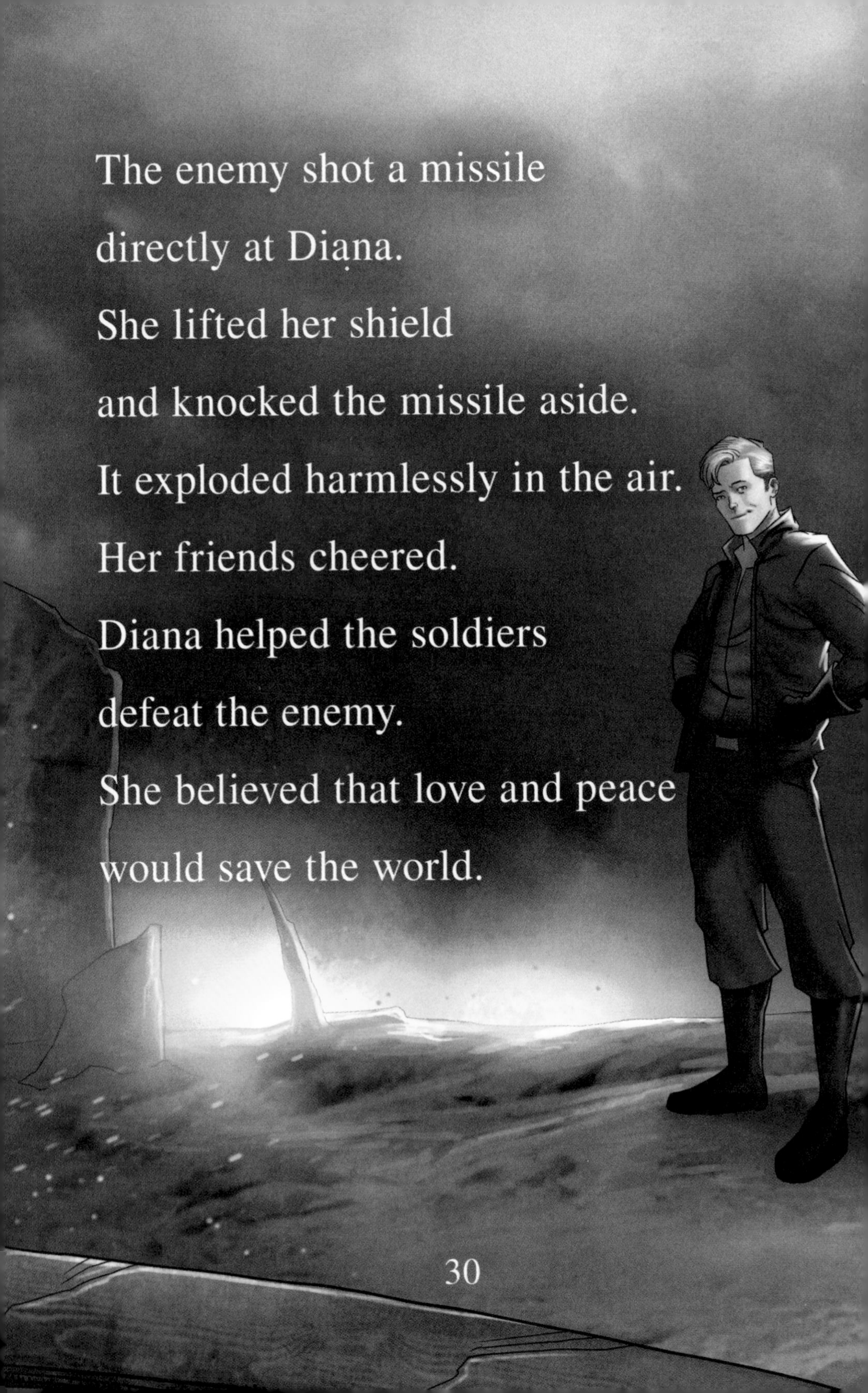

The enemy shot a missile
directly at Diana.
She lifted her shield
and knocked the missile aside.
It exploded harmlessly in the air.
Her friends cheered.
Diana helped the soldiers
defeat the enemy.
She believed that love and peace
would save the world.

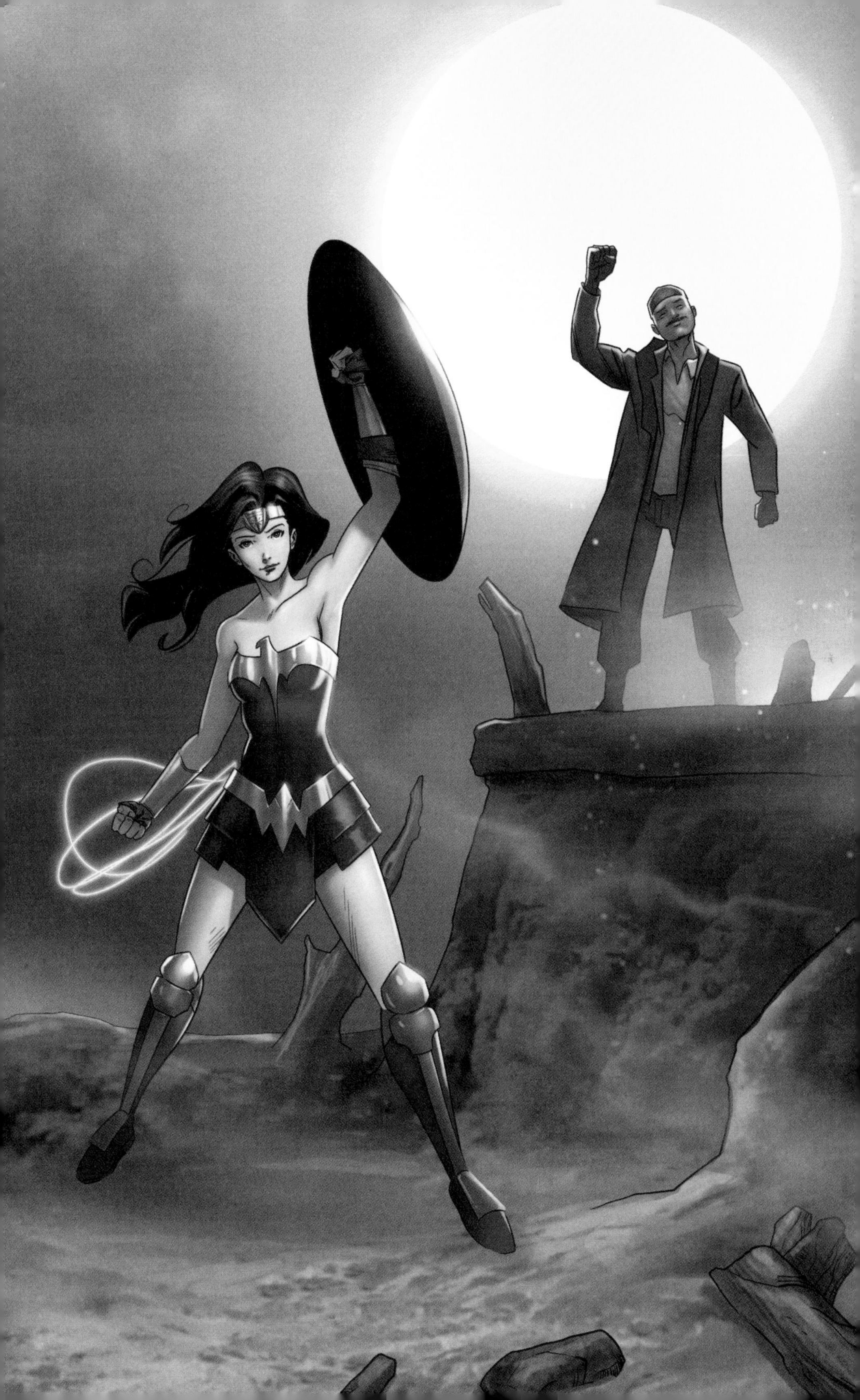

Diana and her friends posed
for a photo.
This was just the beginning of her
journey to become Wonder Woman,
the hero the world needed.

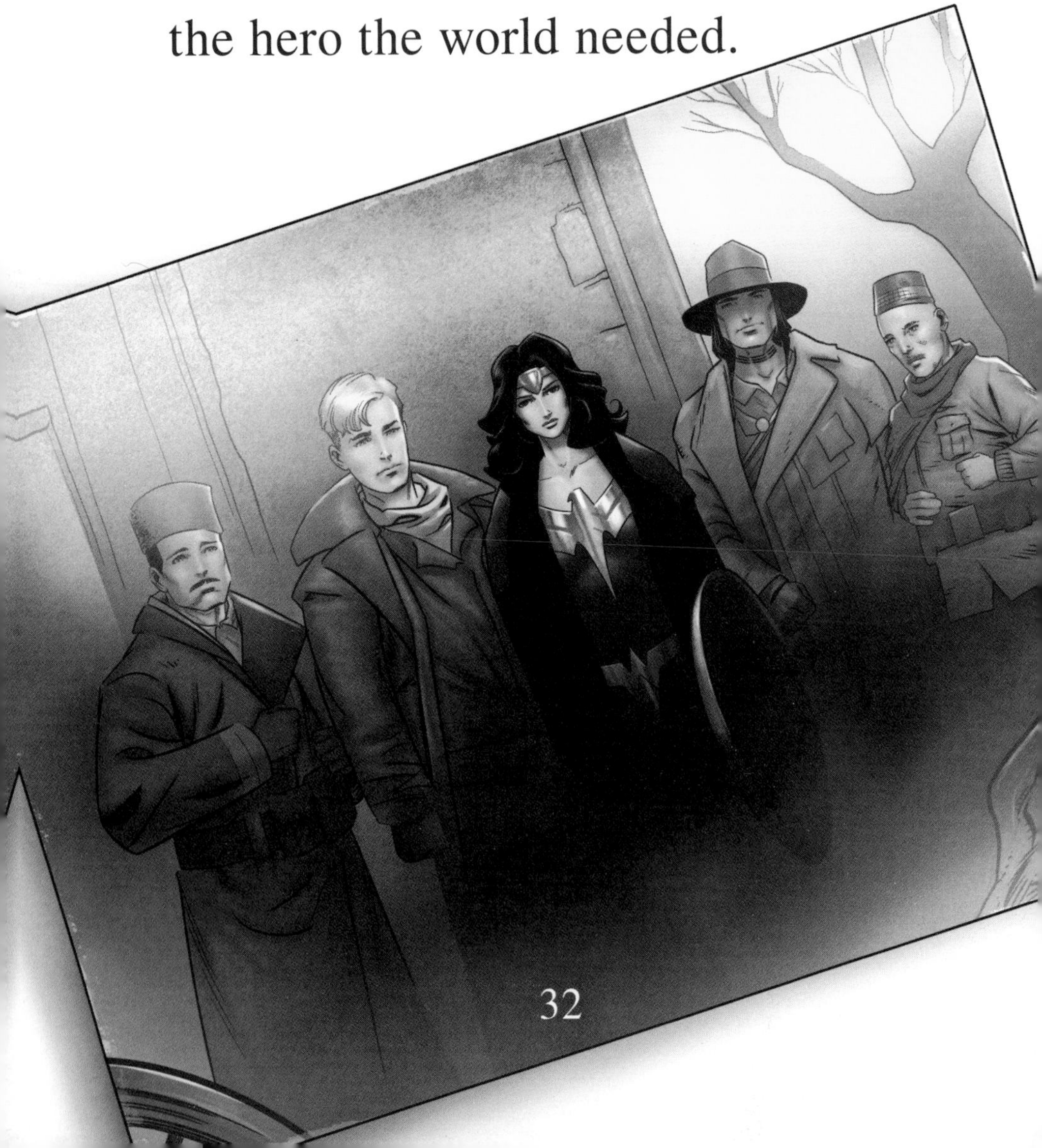